Horrible Haircut

First published in Great Britain 2000 by Mammoth
an imprint of Egmont Children's Books Limited
239 Kensington High Street, London W8 6SA.
Published in hardback by Heinemann Library,
a division of Reed Educational and Professional Publishing Limited
by arrangement with Egmont Children's Books Limited.

Paperback ISBN 0 7497 42666
Hardback ISBN 0 431 06985 9
10 9 8 7 6 5 4 3 2 1
A CIP catalogue record for this title is available from the British Library.
Printed in Dubai.

Horrible Haircut

Alison Ritchie

Illustrated by Ian Newsham

Blue Bananas

To my hairdresser

A.R.

To Wendy and Mint

I.N.

Lucy had long hair. Lucy liked

her long hair.

She liked her hair

long and tangly and messy.

Her mother didn't.

And her father didn't.

'Lucy!' her mum said.

'You look like a hyena.'

'Good!' said Lucy.

'Lucy!' her dad said. 'You look like a baboon!'

'Even better!' said Lucy.

'I think Lucy looks like Scruff!' said Lucy's brother Johnny.

'Perfect!' said Lucy.

'Time for a haircut!' said Mum

and Dad together.

'No! No! No!' said Lucy, running

out of the room and up the stairs.

'Yes! Yes! Yes!' said Lucy's mum,

fetching the scissors.

‘Come on, Lucy!’ Mum shouted.

‘Come downstairs.’

‘No! I don’t want my hair cut!’

‘Come down NOW!’

Oh Mum,
do I have
to?
Oh no!
I'm off!
Me too!

‘Promise you won’t cut off too much?’

said Lucy.

‘I promise!’ said Mum.

‘Promise you’ll stop when I say so?’

said Lucy.

‘I promise!’ said Mum.

‘Promise you’ll make it look nice?’

‘Oh Lucy! Yes! Look, if you don’t like it, then you can cut mine, OK?’

‘I can cut your hair if I don’t like mine?’ asked Lucy. ‘Promise?’

‘PROMISE!’ said Mum.

'I'll only cut this much! Just so it looks neat,' said Mum.

'Mum,' Lucy scowled. 'I told you. I don't want to look neat!' Mum combed Lucy's hair. Then she sprayed it with water, to make it easier to cut.

'Now sit still, keep your head straight and don't make a fuss!'

Mum cut off a little bit of hair.

Mum cut off a little bit more hair.

Mum cut off even more hair.

Johnny tried to

trim Scruff's fur.

He trimmed his ear instead.

Scruff howled very loudly . . .

and very suddenly.

Mum got a fright.

Mum's hand slipped. She cut off a very big chunk of Lucy's hair.

'Oh, Scruff! You made me jump. NOW look what I've done.'

‘What? What have you done, Mum?’ said Lucy.

‘Um, nothing, everything’s just fine. Johnny, leave the dog alone!’

‘Now, let’s see. Um . . . I just need to . . . er . . . sort of even it all up.’

and a little bit more off here.
Ooops!
Oh...
Eeeek!

Lucy looked at the big pile of hair on the floor.

'STOP!' Lucy jumped up. She ran upstairs to look in the bathroom mirror.

Aaaaaaa

Lucy ran into her bedroom and threw herself on the bed.

'Mum! It's horrible! It's awful!
I hate it! What am I going to DO?
I'm not going to school tomorrow.
I'm not going to school ever again.
Everyone will laugh at me.'

'Of course they won't! Don't be silly!'

'Mum! You don't understand!'

'Look, your real friends won't laugh, and if anyone else does, just say your silly old mother cut your hair too short! Anyway, lots of your friends have short hair.'

'But they've always had short hair,'

said Lucy. 'This is new!'

'Well, it's not that bad!

Come on, let's see

what we can do.'

'Now! We could frizz it all up.

Or tie it up

Or mess it up

or even . . . wear a bow!'

'Right! Now I'm cutting your hair,'

Lucy said, dragging Mum downstairs.

‘OK, Mum. Ready?’

‘Well . . . now, Lucy, you see,

the thing is . . .’

‘You said!’

‘Well, yes, sort of, but . . .’

‘You promised!’

'OK! Sit still!' Lucy said. 'Right, here I go.'

There was a loud

SNIP!

Mum jumped up. She raced upstairs.

She screamed.

Dad came running up the stairs.

He looked at Lucy.

'Oh Lucy! Your hair looks

very er . . . um . . . interesting.'

Then he saw Mum. He didn't

know quite what to say.

'How can I go to work tomorrow?' Mum wailed. 'Everyone will laugh at me! What am I going to do?!'

'Don't worry, Mum,' said Lucy. 'It's fine. Just like mine!'

Lucy was beginning to feel a bit better.

‘Oh dear,’ said Dad. ‘I suppose you could wear a hat?’

‘That’s not funny!’ shouted Mum.

‘Come on, Mum. It’s not that bad. Maybe hats *are* a good idea!’

'I know!' said Lucy. 'I've got a better idea!'

HAIRGEL!

HAIRY
GEL

‘Well, what do you think, Lucy?’ said Mum, who was getting used to her new hair.

Lucy grinned, ‘You look like a hyena,’ she said.

‘That’s funny,’ said Mum, ‘so do you.’

‘Hurray!’ said Lucy.

‘Well, honestly! I live in a house full of scruffs!’ Dad laughed.

‘Talking of scruffs, where is that silly dog?’ said Mum.

‘And where’s Johnny?’ said Dad.

Johnny! Scruff! Where are you?
I can see a ta

‘There they are!’ said Dad.

‘I’m sure they’re up to no good!’ said Mum. ‘Come out, you two.’

I'll sort you out!
Johnny looks cool!

u're a
ht sticky
pair!